D1515014

BRAVO, ALBERT!

by **Lori Haskins Houran** • Illustrated by **Deborah Melmon**

THE KANE PRESS / NEW YORK

To Juliana Hanford. Thank you for all your incredible support and expertise. Bravo!—D.M.

Acknowledgments: We wish to thank the following people for their helpful advice and review of the material contained in this book: Susan Longo, Former Early Childhood and Elementary School Teacher, Mamaroneck, NY; and Rebeka Eston Salemi, Kindergarten Teacher, Lincoln School, Lincoln, MA.

Special thanks to Susan Longo and Meagan Branday Susi for providing the Fun Activities in the back of this book.

Library of Congress Cataloging-in-Publication Data

Names: Houran, Lori Haskins, author. | Melmon, Deborah, illustrator.
Title: Bravo, Albert! / by Lori Haskins Houran ; illustrated by Deborah Melmon.
Description: New York : Kane Press, 2017. | Series: Mouse math | Summary:
After learning about patterns while helping Grandma make a quilt,
Albert the mouse spots patterns everywhere.
Identifiers: LCCN 2016037417 (print) | LCCN 2016047991 (ebook) |
ISBN 9781575658568 (reinforced library binding : alk. paper) |
ISBN 9781575658599 (pbk. : alk. paper) | ISBN 9781575658629 (ebook)
Subjects: | CYAC: Pattern perception—Fiction. | Mice—Fiction.
Classification: LCC PZ7.H27645 Br 2017 (print) | LCC PZ7.H27645 (ebook) | DDC
[E]—dc23
LC record available at https://lccn.loc.gov/2016037417

1 3 5 7 9 10 8 6 4 2

First published in the United States of America in 2017 by Kane Press, Inc.
Printed in China

Book Design: Edward Miller

Mouse Math is a registered trademark of Kane Press, Inc.

Visit us online at **www.kanepress.com**

 Like us on Facebook
facebook.com/kanepress

 Follow us on Twitter
@KanePress

Dear Parent/Educator,

"I can't do math." Every child (or grownup!) who says these words has at some point along the way felt intimidated by math. For young children who are just being introduced to the subject, we wanted to create a world in which math was not simply numbers on a page, but a part of life—an adventure!

Enter Albert and Wanda, two little mice who live in the walls of a People House. Children will be swept along with this irrepressible duo and their merry band of friends as they tackle mouse-sized problems and dilemmas (and sometimes *cat-sized* problems and dilemmas!).

Each book in the **MOUSE MATH**® series provides a fresh take on a basic math concept. The mice discover solutions as they, for instance, use position words while teaching a pet snail to do tricks or count the alarmingly large number of friends they've invited over on a rainy day—and, lo and behold, they are doing math!

Math educators who specialize in early childhood learning have applied their expertise to make sure each title is as helpful as possible to young children—and to their parents and teachers. Fun activities at the ends of the books and on our website encourage kids to think and talk about math in ways that will make each concept clear and memorable.

As with our award-winning Math Matters® series, our aim is to captivate children's imaginations by drawing them into the story, and so into the math at the heart of each adventure. It is our hope that kids will want to hear and read the **MOUSE MATH** stories again and again and that, as they grow up, they will approach math with enthusiasm and see it as an invaluable tool for navigating the world they live in.

Sincerely,

Joanne Kane

Joanne E. Kane
Publisher

MOUSE MATH titles:

Albert Adds Up!
Adding/Taking Away

Albert Doubles the Fun
Adding Doubles

Albert Helps Out
Counting Money

Albert Is NOT Scared
Direction Words

Albert Keeps Score
Comparing Numbers

Albert's Amazing Snail
Position Words

Albert's BIGGER Than Big Idea
Comparing Sizes: Big/Small

Albert Starts School
Days of the Week

Albert the Muffin-Maker
Ordinal Numbers

A Beach for Albert
Capacity

Bravo, Albert!
Patterns

Count Off, Squeak Scouts!
Number Sequence

If the Shoe Fits
Nonstandard Units of Measurement

Lost in the Mouseum
Left/Right

Make a Wish, Albert!
3D Shapes

Mice on Ice
2D Shapes

The Mousier the Merrier!
Counting

A Mousy Mess
Sorting

The Right Place for Albert
One-to-One Correspondence

Where's Albert?
Counting & Skip Counting

"Hey, Wanda! Want to play checkers?" asked Albert.

"Sorry," Wanda said. "I'm super busy."

Albert sighed. Wanda was *always* super busy since she started her singing group, the Nibblettes.

"I have to pick our costumes for the show tomorrow!" said Wanda. "Hmm. Purple or pink?"

"Pur—" Albert began.

Too late! Wanda had already grabbed the phone.
"Abby, let's wear the pink shirts! No—the purple ones . . ."

Albert sighed again. *I wonder if Grandma wants company.*

Albert scootered to Grandma's house.

"I was just wishing for an extra set of paws!" said Grandma.
"I'm making a quilt. Will you pass me the squares?"

Albert saw two stacks of soft cloth squares.
"Yellow and green. My favorite colors!"

He passed a yellow square to Grandma. Then another one.

"Oops!" Grandma said. "I need green next. See the pattern? Yellow, green, yellow, green."

"Why do you do it like that?" Albert wondered.

"A pattern makes the quilt nice and neat. Look what happens if I *don't* use one."

Grandma plopped down some squares. A green, a few yellows, more greens, a yellow.

"It's . . . kind of messy," Albert said.

"Exactly," Grandma agreed. "And I want my quilt to show that I put lots of care into it."

Albert passed Grandma the rest of the squares in just the right order. "Yellow, green, yellow, green," he told himself.

When Albert left Grandma's house, he started spotting patterns everywhere!

The stripes on the candy shop awning went red, blue, red, blue.

The polka dots on Mrs. Gouda's hat went orange, brown, orange, brown.

The flowers in front of the post office were all white, but they made a pattern, too! Tulips, daisies, tulips, daisies.

Back home, Albert found Wanda in their room.
She was super busy, of course.

"I want the Nibblettes to match perfectly," she said.
"I'm making us matching necklaces!"

"Can I help?" asked Albert.

"Sure." Wanda slid over two bins. One held heart-shaped beads, the other butterflies.

Albert started stringing beads. *I'll follow a pattern so the necklace looks nice,* he decided.

Butterfly, heart, butterfly, heart . . .

"Wait," said Wanda. "I forgot to tell you the pattern!"

"Don't worry. I already used one." Albert held up his string proudly.

"That's pretty, Albert. But I'm following a different pattern. Watch."

Wanda slid a butterfly onto her string, then a heart, and *another* heart! She made the pattern again. Butterfly, heart, heart.

"Oh! Two hearts in a row. Got it!" Albert said.
Soon they had a dozen necklaces—one for each Nibblette.

"What do you think?" asked Wanda the next morning. Her necklace glittered against her pink shirt.

"You look great!" Albert put the other necklaces in his backpack. "Let's go to the show!"

The theater was already filling up with mice.
Albert waved to Grandma in the front row.

"What a crowd," said Wanda, beaming.

THE NIBBLETTES

But when she got backstage, Wanda gasped.

Some of the Nibblettes were wearing pink shirts, like her.
Some were wearing purple. Some were wearing *orange*!

"It's my fault!" Wanda wailed. "I kept changing my mind.
Now we don't match. We'll look messy on stage!"

Messy?

Albert remembered what Grandma said about her quilt.
A pattern makes it nice and neat.

Squares could make a pattern. Beads could make a
pattern . . .

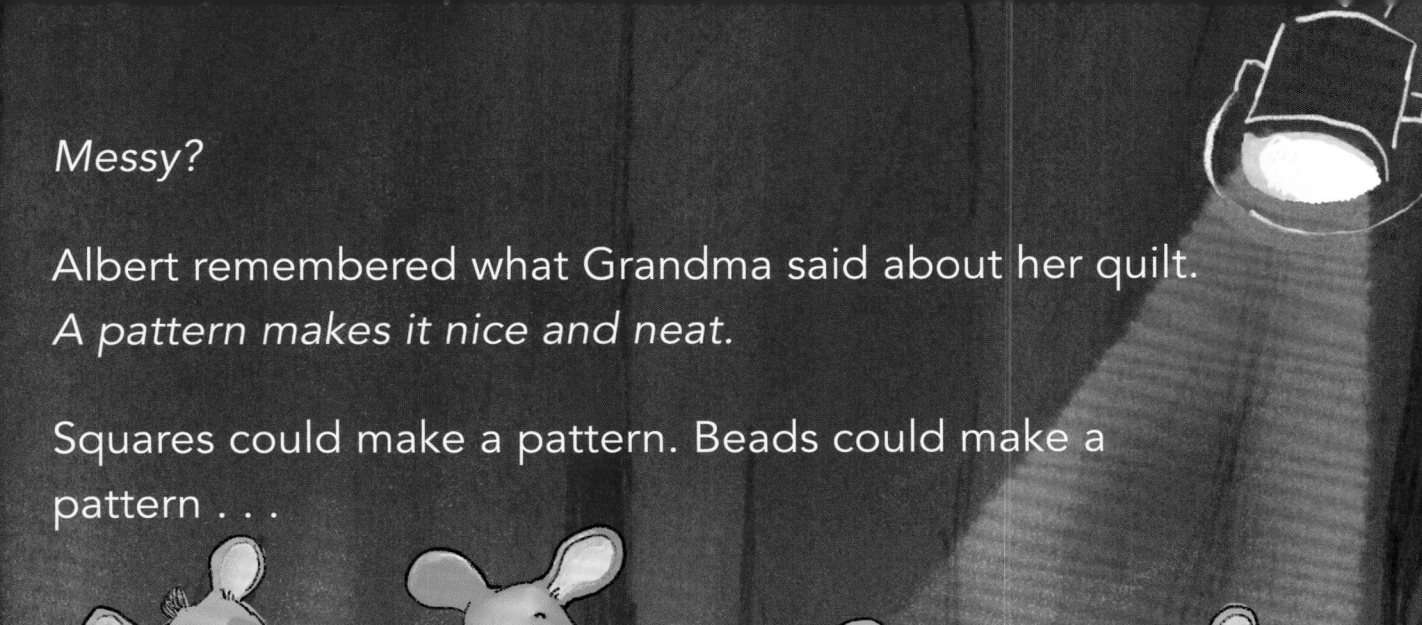

"Wanda!" cried Albert. "The Nibblettes could make a pattern! Then you wouldn't look messy at all!"

Albert started zipping around. There were three colors to use, so it would be tricky. But he was sure he could do it.

"Orange, pink, purple," he said, lining up the singers.
"Orange, pink, purple."

It was working!

Then Albert got to the end of the line. There were too many purple Nibblettes left over!

"It's almost show time!" squeaked Wanda. "And we still have to hand out the necklaces!"

The necklaces! Albert pulled them out of his backpack.

Butterfly, heart, heart. Two hearts in a row . . .
That was it!

Albert raced around again. This time he tossed the Nibblettes their necklaces as they got in line. And he put *two* purple Nibblettes in a row!

"Orange, purple, purple, pink. Orange, purple, purple, pink. Orange, purple, purple, AND . . ."

Albert tugged Wanda to the end of the line. "Pink!"

He wiped his forehead. *Phew!*

"Albert, you did it!" Wanda shouted, just as the curtain flew up!

"Bravo! The Nibblettes were fantastic!" said Grandma after the show. She gave Wanda a big bouquet of flowers.

Wanda grinned. "Thanks, Grandma!"

"Bravo to you, too." Grandma passed Albert a box.

"This is for you. Something tells me you might want it as soon as you get home."

Sure enough . . .

Grandma was right!

FUN ACTIVITIES

Bravo, Albert! supports children's understanding of **identifying and formulating patterns**, important topics in early math learning. Use the activities below to extend the math topic and to reinforce children's early reading skills.

 ENGAGE

▶ Read the title aloud and examine the cover. Ask children if they have ever heard the word *bravo* before. Encourage the children to discuss where they have heard it and what they think it means. Based on their discussion, model a prediction about what might occur in the story. Have students explain whether they agree or disagree with your prediction.

▶ Talk about what a pattern is and ask children to share patterns that they have seen.

▶ Instruct children to be on the lookout for patterns as you read the story.

LOOK BACK

▶ Review the story and illustrations and ask students to point out the patterns they noticed while you were reading. Discuss the different types of patterns that were included in the book.

▶ Ask: *Aside from the patterns that were a part of the story itself, did you spot any other patterns in the illustrations? (Hint: Look closely at pages 3, 14, 19, 26, and 30.)*

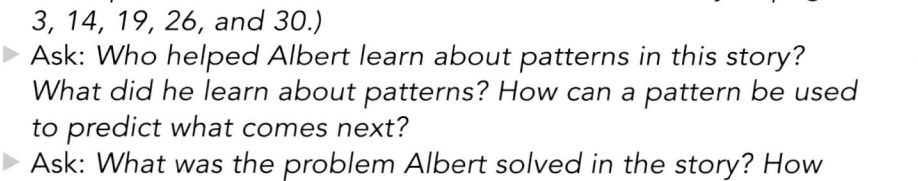

▶ Ask: *Who helped Albert learn about patterns in this story? What did he learn about patterns? How can a pattern be used to predict what comes next?*

▶ Ask: *What was the problem Albert solved in the story? How was he able to use what he learned about patterns to solve the problem?*

▶ Reexamine the title of the book and ask children to explain why they think the author chose that title for the book.

TRY THIS!

We're Going on a Pattern Hunt!

▶ Provide small groups of children with clipboards, paper, and crayons or colored pencils. Instruct children that they will become "Pattern Detectives" and will set out to discover and record any patterns they come across!

▶ Begin by searching in the classroom for any patterns and then proceed to the rest of the school building and the outdoor playground.

▶ Encourage children to take their time recording the patterns they see and to try to copy them down as they see them. Reinforce that patterns exist not only in colors but also in shapes and designs.

▶ Once children have had a chance to be detectives and discover patterns, return to the classroom and have them take turns sharing their discoveries.

THINK!

Pattern Superstars

▶ Give children circles and stars (these can be stickers or cut out shapes).

▶ Tell children to create patterns using those two shapes.

▶ Ask children to share their patterns and explain them to the whole group.

▶ Display the patterns that were created and ask children to look for patterns that are similar and to explain how they are alike.

▶ Add heart shapes and ask students to create a pattern using all three shapes.

▶ Again, have children share their patterns, display them, and discuss their similarities.

▶ **Bonus**: Create a pattern using **12** circles, **4** stars, and **8** hearts. (Children must use all of the shapes in their patterns, just like Albert had to include all the members of the Nibblettes.)

◆ **FOR MORE ACTIVITIES** ◆

visit **www.kanepress.com/mouse-math-activities**